U0032470

Four
Quartets

四重奏

T. S. Eliot

杜國清 譯

CONTENTS

Burnt Norton

焚毀的諾頓[1]

〈 四重奏 〉之一

Burnt Norton
No.1 of 'Four Quartets'

τοῦ λόγου δὲ ἐόντος ξυνοῦ ζώουσιν οἱ πολλοί

ὡς ἰδίαν ἔχοντες φρόνησιν.

ὁδὸς ἄνω κάτω μία καὶ ὡυτή.

——Diels: *Die Fragmente der Vorsokratiker (Herakleitos).*

焚毀的諾頓
〈四重奏〉之一

雖說「道」是萬人共通的原則，大多數人活著似乎都有自我的理解力。

上行道與下行道同是一條路。

   —— Diels 編：《蘇格拉底時代哲學者的片斷》

Burnt Norton
No.1 of 'Four Quartets'

I

5. Time present and time past

Are both perhaps present in time future,

And time future contained in time past.

If all time is eternally present

All time is unredeemable

10. What might have been is an abstraction

Remaining a perpetual possibility

Only in a world of speculation.

What might have been and what has been

Point to one end, which is always present.

15. Footfalls echo in the memory

Down the passage which we did not take

Towards the door we never opened

焚毀的諾頓
〈四重奏〉之一

I

5. 時間現在與時間過去

二者或許存在於時間未來，

而時間未來包含在時間過去中。

假如一切時間永遠存在

一切時間都無可贖回。

10. 可能曾經有過的是一種抽象

留下永遠的可能性，

只存在於思索的世界中。

可能曾經有過的，以及曾經有過的

指向一個終點，那永遠是現在。

15. 足音在記憶中迴響

沿著我們沒走過的通道

向著我們沒開過的門

Burnt Norton
No.1 of 'Four Quartets'

Into the rose-garden. My words echo

Thus, in your mind.

20.   But to what purpose

Disturbing the dust on a bowl of rose-leaves

I do not know.

Other echoes

Inhabit the garden. Shall we follow?

25. Quick, said the bird, find them, find them,

Round the corner. Through the first gate,

Into our first world, shall we follow

The deception of the thrush? Into our first world.

There they were, dignified, invisible,

30. Moving without pressure, over the dead leaves,

In the autumn heat, through the vibrant air,

And the bird called, in response to

焚毀的諾頓
〈四重奏〉之一

進入玫瑰花園。我的話

如此，回響在你的心中。

20.　　　　　　　　但是為了什麼目的

騷擾一盆玫瑰葉上的塵埃

我不知道。

　　　　其他種種回響

棲息在這花園裡。我們跟著去嗎？

25.　快快，小鳥說，把它們找出來，把它們找出來，

就在那拐角兒。穿過第一道門，

進入我們的最初世界，我們要跟隨

那隻畫眉的欺矇嗎？進入我們的最初世界。

就在那兒，顯得高貴，但看不見，

30.　沒有壓力地移動，越過枯葉

在秋暖中，穿過顫動的空氣，

於是小鳥叫了，應和著

Burnt Norton
No.1 of 'Four Quartets'

The unheard music hidden in the shrubbery,

And the unseen eyebeam crossed, for the roses

35. Had the look of flowers that are looked at.

There they were as our guests, accepted and accepting.

So we moved, and they, in a formal pattern,

Along the empty alley, into the box circle,

To look down into the drained pool.

40. Dry the pool, dry concrete, brown edged,

And the pool was filled with water out of sunlight,

And the lotos rose, quietly, quietly,

The surface glittered out of heart of light,

And they were behind us, reflected in the pool.

45. Then a cloud passed, and the pool was empty.

Go, said the bird, for the leaves were full of children,

Hidden excitedly, containing laughter.

焚毀的諾頓
〈四重奏〉之一

灌木中隱然聽不見的音樂

而看不見的眼神交叉，因為玫瑰

35. 具有引人觀賞的花容。

就在那裡，像我們的客人，招待也被招待。

於是我們行動，他們也一樣，以正式的模樣，

沿著無人的小路，走進黃楊樹的圓圈，

向下望著沒有水的池塘。

40. 乾涸的池塘，乾涸的水泥，褐色的邊緣，

而池塘充滿陽光照射的水，

而水蓮升起，靜靜地，靜靜地，

池面在陽光的中心閃耀著，

這些都在我們背後，映照在池塘裡。

45. 然後一片雲飄過，而池塘空空。

去吧，小鳥說，到那邊，葉蔭下滿是小孩，

興奮地隱藏著，忍住笑聲。

Go, go, go, said the bird: human kind

Cannot bear very much reality.

50. Time past and time future

What might have been and what has been

Point to one end, which is always present.

焚毀的諾頓
〈 四重奏 〉之一

去吧，去吧，去吧，小鳥說，人類
不堪忍受太多的現實。

50. 時間過去與時間未來
可能曾經有過的以及曾經有過的
指向一個終點，那永遠是現在。

Burnt Norton
No.1 of 'Four Quartets'

II

Garlic and sapphires in the mud

Clot the bedded axle-tree.

55. The trilling wire in the blood

Sings below inveterate scars

Appeasing long forgotten wars.

The dance along the artery

The circulation of the lymph

60. Are figured in the drift of stars

Ascend to summer in the tree

We move above the moving tree

In light upon the figured leaf

And hear upon the sodden floor

65. Below, the boarhound and the boar

焚毀的諾頓

〈四重奏〉之一

II

泥沼中的大蒜與藍寶石

凝結在被埋置的輪軸上。

55. 血液中顫動的金絲

在痼疾的傷痕底下歌唱

平息久被遺忘的爭戰。

沿著動脈的舞蹈

淋巴腺的循環

60. 在群星的漂移中成形

攀升到樹中的夏天

我們移動在移動的樹上方

在有花紋模樣的葉子上的光中

且在潮濕的地面底下

65. 聽到野豬獵犬和野豬

Burnt Norton
No.1 of 'Four Quartets'

Pursue their pattern as before

But reconciled among the stars.

At the still point of the turning world. Neither flesh nor

fleshless;

Neither from nor towards; at the still point, there the dance is,

70. But neither arrest nor movement. And do not call it fixity,

Where past and future are gathered. Neither movement from

nor towards,

Neither ascent nor decline. Except for the point, the still

point,

There would be no dance, and there is only the dance.

I can only say, there we have been: but I cannot say where.

75. And I cannot say, how long, for that is to place it in time.

焚毀的諾頓

〈四重奏〉之一

爭相追逐自己的模型一如從前

但在繁星中獲得了和解。

在流轉的世界中那靜點。不是肉體也不是非肉體；

不是來自也不是歸向；在那靜止點，舞蹈就在那裡，

70. 但不是停止也不是移動。那不叫做固定，

在那裡過去與未來集合在一起。移動不是來自那裡，也不

是歸向那裡，

不是上升也不是下降。除了那個點，那個靜止點之外

不會有舞蹈，因而只有舞蹈在那裡。

我只能說：我們一直在那裡：但我說不出在哪裡。

75. 而且我說不出，已有多久，因那樣也就將它置於時間中。

Burnt Norton
No.1 of 'Four Quartets'

The inner freedom from the practical desire,

The release from action and suffering, release from the inner

And the outer compulsion, yet surrounded

By a grace of sense, a white light still and moving,

80.   Erhebung without motion, concentration

Without elimination, both a new world

And the old made explicit, understood

In the completion of its partial ecstasy,

The resolution of its partial horror.

85.   Yet the enchainment of past and future

Woven in the weakness of the changing body,

Protects mankind from heaven and damnation

Which flesh cannot endure.

                              Time past and time future

90.   Allow but a little consciousness.

焚毀的諾頓

〈四重奏〉之一

　　　　來自現實欲望的內在自由，

從行動與受苦中獲得的解脫，從內在

與外在強迫中獲得的解脫，然而

由於感官的福報，被靜止而移動的白光所包圍，

80. 沒有動作的高揚，沒有排除的

專注，讓新的和舊的世界

兩者都變明確，可以被理解，

在部分狂喜的完成中，

部分恐怖的解除中。

85. 然而過去與未來的連結

由身體無常的弱點所織成

保護著人類免遭天堂和地獄的詛咒

那是肉體所難以忍受的。

　　　　　　　　　時間過去與時間未來

90. 只容許些微的意識。

To be conscious is not to be in time

But only in time can the moment in the rose-garden,

The moment in the arbour where the rain beat,

The moment in the draughty church at smokefall

95. Be remembered; involved with past and future.

Only through time time is conquered.

焚毀的諾頓
〈四重奏〉之一

意識的存在不存在時間中

但是只有在時間中，在玫瑰園中的瞬間

在雨打園亭中的瞬間，

在下霧時通風的教堂中的瞬間

95.　才被人想起；涉及到過去與未來。

只有透過時間，時間才被征服。

III

Here is a place of disaffection

Time before and time after

In a dim light: neither daylight

100. Investing form with lucid stillness

Turning shadow into transient beauty

With slow rotation suggesting permanence

Nor darkness to purify the soul

Emptying the sensual with deprivation

105. Cleansing affection from the temporal.

Neither plenitude nor vacancy. Only a flicker

Over the strained time-ridden faces

Distracted from distraction by distraction

Filled with fancies and empty of meaning

焚毀的諾頓
〈四重奏〉之一

III

這裡是一個憤懣的地方

時間以前與時間以後

在朦朧的光中：既不是日光

100. 以明亮的靜止附與形體

以暗示久遠的緩慢旋轉

將暗影轉成無常的美，

也不是藉以淨化靈魂的黑黯，

以剝奪清空官能的世界

105. 清洗感情中現世的一切。

既不是充實也不是空虛。只是一閃

掠過時間驅使下緊繃的臉

因分心而心煩意亂的那些臉

充滿幻想和意義的空虛

110. Tumid apathy with no concentration

Men and bits of paper, whirled by the cold wind

That blows before and after time,

Wind in and out of unwholesome lungs

Time before and time after.

115. Eructation of unhealthy souls

Into the faded air, the torpid

Driven on the wind that sweeps the gloomy hills of London,

Hampstead and Clerkenwell, Campden and Putney,

Highgate, Primrose and Ludgate. Not here

120. Not here the darkness, in this twittering world.

Descend lower, descend only

Into the world of perpetual solitude,

World not world, but that which is not world,

焚毀的諾頓
〈四重奏〉之一

110. 無所專注的腫起的冷漠無感

人們與報紙碎片，被冷風吹起

在時間之前和時間之後迴舞，

不健全的肺部所吐納的風

在過去和未來的時間中。

115. 不健康的靈魂的噯氣

吐入稀薄的空氣中，那些麻木不仁的

隨風吹趕，掃過倫敦陰鬱的山丘，

漢普斯鐵和克拉肯威爾，肯普頓和帕特尼，

海格特，普林露色和路德格特。

120. 黑黯不在這裡，不在這嘈嚷不休的世界。

再往下走，一路往下

向著永恆的孤獨世界，

非世界的世界，但那不是世界，

Burnt Norton
No.1 of 'Four Quartets'

Internal darkness, deprivation

125. And destitution of all property,

Desiccation of the world of sense,

Evacuation of the world of fancy,

Inoperancy of the world of spirit;

This is the one way, and the other

130. Is the same, not in movement

But abstention from movement; while the world moves

In appetency, on its metalled ways

Of time past and time future.

焚毀的諾頓
〈四重奏〉之一

　　向著內部的黑闇，

125.　向著所有財產的剝奪和貧乏，

　　向著感官世界的枯竭，

　　向著幻想世界的撤離，

　　向著精神世界的癱瘓；

　　這是一個方法，另一個

130.　也是一樣，不在動中

　　而在動的戒絕中；然而這世界移動著

　　在欲望的本能中，在自己的

　　時間過去與時間未來的軌道上。

Burnt Norton
No.1 of 'Four Quartets'

IV

Time and the bell have buried the day,

135. The black cloud carries the sun away.

Will the sunflower turn to us, will the clematis

Stray down, bend to us; tendril and spray

Clutch and cling?

Chill

140. Fingers of yew be curled

Down on us? After the kingfisher's wing

Has answered light to light, and is silent, the light is still

At the still point of the turning world.

焚毀的諾頓
〈四重奏〉之一

IV

時間與晚鐘埋葬了一日，

135. 黑雲帶走了太陽。

向日葵會轉向我們嗎，鐵線蓮

會迷途，彎向我們；藤蔓和細枝

會緊抓纏住我們嗎？

冷冷的

140. 紫杉樹的手指會捲曲

垂向我們嗎？在翡翠鳥的羽翼

——回應了光而沉默之後，光靜止

在這輪轉世界的靜止點上。

Burnt Norton
No.1 of 'Four Quartets'

V

Words move, music moves

145. Only in time; but that which is only living

Can only die. Words, after speech, reach

Into the silence. Only by the form, the pattern,

Can words or music reach

The stillness, as a Chinese jar still

150. Moves perpetually in its stillness.

Not the stillness of the violin, while the note lasts,

Not that only, but the co-existence,

Or say that the end precedes the beginning,

And the end and the beginning were always there

155. Before the beginning and after the end.

And all is always now. Words strain,

焚毀的諾頓
〈四重奏〉之一

V

言語移動，音樂移動

145. 只在時間中；但是只有活的東西

才能死去。言語，在說出之後

到達沉默。只有藉著形式和樣型，

言語與音樂才能

到達靜止，像靜止的中國花瓶

150. 永遠在靜止中移動。

只要餘音還在，就不是梵哦玲的靜止，

不僅如此，而且是共存，

或者說結束存在於開始之前，

而結束和開始恆常在那裡

155. 在開始之前，在結束之後。

而一切恆是現在。言語緊繃，

Burnt Norton
No.1 of 'Four Quartets'

Crack and sometimes break, under the burden,

Under the tension, slip, slide, perish,

Decay with imprecision, will not stay in place,

160. Will not stay still. Shrieking voices

Scolding, mocking, or merely chattering,

Always assail them. The Word in the desert

Is most attacked by voices of temptation,

The crying shadow in the funeral dance,

165. The loud lament of the disconsolate chimera.

The detail of the pattern is movement,

As in the figure of the ten stairs.

Desire itself is movement

Not in itself desirable;

170. Love is itself unmoving,

焚毀的諾頓
〈四重奏〉之一

有時震裂或折斷，在重荷之下，

張力之下溜動，滑倒，淪喪，

因不精確而腐敗，不會停留在一處，

160. 不會靜止不動。尖叫的聲音

責罵，嘲笑，或只是閑聊，

經常攻擊言語。曠野中主的話

最受誘惑的聲音襲擊，

葬禮的舞蹈中哭泣的影子，

165. 哀傷的怪獸高聲的慟哭。

樣型的細節是動，

有如十級階梯的形態。

欲望本身是動

它本身並不令人欲望；

170. 愛本身是不動的

Only the cause and end of movement,

Timeless, and undesiring

Except in the aspect of time

Caught in the form of limitation

175. Between un-being and being.

Sudden in a shaft of sunlight

Even while the dust moves

There rises the hidden laughter

Of children in the foliage

180. Quick now, here, now, always—

Ridiculous the waste sad time

Stretching before and after.

焚毀的諾頓
〈四重奏〉之一

只是動的原因和目的，

超時間，而且非欲望的，

除非以時間的樣相

以具有侷限性的形態

175. 被夾在非存在與存在之間。

突然在一柱陽光中

甚至當塵埃移動時

隱藏在葉叢中

一群小孩的笑聲揚起，

180. 現在趕快，這裡，現在，隨時——

荒謬的是那徒然悲傷的時間

在之前和之後不斷延伸。

Burnt Norton
No.1 of 'Four Quartets'

---

1   譯註:焚毀的諾頓指位於英格蘭北諾頓 Gloucestershire 郡的一座英國
     鄉間住宅,有玫瑰園遺址。

· No.2 ·

East Coker

東科克[1]

〈四重奏〉之二

East Coker
No.2 of 'Four Quartets'

I

In my beginning is my end. In succession

Houses rise and fall, crumble, are extended,

Are removed, destroyed, restored, or in their place

Is an open field, or a factory, or a by-pass.

5. Old stone to new building, old timber to new fires,

Old fires to ashes, and ashes to the earth

Which is already flesh, fur and faeces,

Bone of man and beast, cornstalk and leaf.

Houses live and die: there is a time for building

10. And a time for living and for generation

And a time for the wind to break the loosened pan

And to shake the wainscot where the field-mouse trots

And to shake the tattered arras woven with a silent motto.

東科克
〈四重奏〉之二

I

　　我的開始裡有我的結束。連續不斷地

　　房子建起又倒塌，粉碎，被擴建

　　被移走，破壞，重建，或者在原地

　　變成曠野，或工廠，或開路。

5.　　從舊石頭到新建築，舊木材到新火焰，

　　舊火焰到灰燼，而灰燼到大地

　　地上早有肉身，皮毛和糞便，

　　人和動物的骸骨，玉米稈和樹葉。

　　房屋活過，死去：有建造的時間

10.　　有活存的時間，跨過世代

　　有時間讓風吹破鬆懈的嵌板，

　　震動野鼠奔竄的壁板，

　　震動掛在壁上織有沉默箴言的破毯。

East Coker
No.2 of 'Four Quartets'

In my beginning is my end. Now the light falls

15. Across the open field, leaving the deep lane

Shuttered with branches, dark in the afternoon,

Where you lean against a bank while a van passes,

And the deep lane insists on the direction

Into the village, in the electric heat

20. Hypnotised. In a warm haze the sultry light

Is absorbed, not refracted, by grey stone.

The dahlias sleep in the empty silence.

Wait for the early owl.

In that open field

25. If you do not come too close, if you do not come too close,

On a summer midnight, you can hear the music

Of the weak pipe and the little drum

東科克
〈四重奏〉之二

我的開始裡有我的結束。這時陽光落下

15. 橫過曠野,使得在樹枝的遮蔭下的

深長小路,在午後顯得陰暗,

在那兒你靠向土堤,當一輛卡車經過,

而濃蔭的小路堅持伸向

村落的方向,處於電熱的

20. 催眠狀態。在暖暖的霧靄中

悶熱的陽光被灰岩吸收,而不是折射。

大麗花在空虛的無聲中沉睡。

等待早來的貓頭鷹。

在那原野中

25. 假如你不走得太近,假如你不走得太近,

在一個夏日夜半,你可以聽到

微弱的笛聲和小鼓的音樂,

East Coker
No.2 of 'Four Quartets'

And see them dancing around the bonfire

The association of man and woman

30. In daunsinge, signifying matrimonie—

A dignified and commodiois sacrament.

Two and two, necessarye coniunction,

Holding eche other by the hand or the arm

Whiche betokeneth concorde. Round and round the fire

35. Leaping through the flames, or joined in circles,

Rustically solemn or in rustic laughter

Lifting heavy feet in clumsy shoes,

Earth feet, loam feet, lifted in country mirth

Mirth of those long since under earth

40. Nourishing the corn. Keeping time,

Keeping the rhythm in their dancing

As in their living in the living seasons—

東科克
〈四重奏〉之二

且看見他們圍著篝火舞蹈

男女互相交往

30. 兩人共舞，意味著結婚——

莊嚴而綽約的聖禮。

兩兩成雙，天作之合，

手牽手　臂交臂

表示琴瑟和諧。圍著繞著篝火

35. 躍過火焰，或加入繞圈，

鄉土氣的莊嚴或在純樸的笑聲中

舉起笨重的腳，穿著笨拙的鞋子

沾泥的腳，沃土的腳，在鄉村的歡樂中舉起

那是長久以來在地底下

40. 滋養穀物那些人的歡笑。跟著節拍

跟著他們舞蹈的節奏

如他們跟著生活季節的生活

East Coker
No.2 of 'Four Quartets'

The time of the seasons and the constellations

The time of milking and the time of harvest

45. The time of the coupling of man and woman

And that of beasts. Feet rising and falling

Eating and drinking. Dung and death.

Dawn points, and another day

Prepares for heat and silence. Out at sea the dawn wind

50. Wrinkles and slides. I am here

Or there, or elsewhere. In my beginning.

東科克
〈四重奏〉之二

季節和星座的時節

擠奶的時節，收穫的時節

45. 男人和女人交媾的時節

還有動物的時節。腳舉起又落下。

飲食男女。糞便和死亡。

東方既白，又是另一天

為暑熱和無言作準備。在那海上黎明的風

50. 吹起皺紋滑行。我在這兒

或在那兒，或者哪兒也不在。在我的開始中。

East Coker
No.2 of 'Four Quartets'

II

What is the late November doing

With the disturbance of the spring

And creatures of the summer heat,

55. And snowdrops writhing under feet

And hollyhocks that aim too high

Red into grey and tumble down

Late roses filled with early snow?

Thunder rolled by the rolling stars

60. Simulates triumphal cars

Deployed in constellated wars

Scorpion fights against the Sun

Until the Sun and Moon go down

Comets weep and Leonids fly

東科克
〈四重奏〉之二

II

歲時十一月末，

有何關聯：與春天的騷動

以及盛夏的生物，

55.　以及在腳下折騰的雪花蓮、

以及嚮往過高、由紅轉灰

而墜落的蜀葵，

沾滿初雪晚開的玫瑰？

因迴旋的流星而迴響的雷聲

60.　猶如凱旋的戰車

在星際大戰中所展開的

天蠍座與太陽相搏

直到日落，月沉

彗星哭泣而獅子座流星雨橫飛

65. Hunt the heavens and the plains

Whirled in a vortex that shall bring

The world to that destructive fire

Which burns before the ice-cap reigns.

That was a way of putting it—not very satisfactory:

70. A periphrastic study in a worn-out poetical fashion,

Leaving one still with the intolerable wrestle

With words and meanings. The poetry does not matter.

It was not (to start again) what one had expected.

What was to be the value of the long looked forward to,

75. Long hoped for calm, the autumnal serenity

And the wisdom of age? Had they deceived us

Or deceived themselves, the quiet-voiced elders,

Bequeathing us merely a receipt for deceit?

東科克
〈四重奏〉之二

65. 獵尋天宇和原野

捲入一個漩渦，將這世界

帶向毀滅的火焰

不斷燃燒直到冰河統領一切。

可以這麼說──雖不滿意：

70. 陳腐詩論的迂言法研究，

仍然留給人、與字句和意義

難以忍受的角力。這種詩無關重要。

這不是（再說一遍）人們所曾期待的。

長久期待的東西，

75. 長久希望的平靜，秋天的安祥

以及老年的智慧，會有什麼價值？

說話低聲的長者矇騙了我們，或是矇騙了他們自己，

而遺留給我們的只是受騙的收據？

The serenity only a deliberate hebetude,

80. The wisdom only the knowledge of dead secrets

Useless in the darkness into which they peered

Or from which they turned their eyes. There is, it seems to us,

At best, only a limited value

In the knowledge derived from experience.

85. The knowledge imposes a pattern, and falsifies,

For the pattern is new in every moment

And every moment is a new and shocking

Valuation of all we have been. We are only undeceived

Of that which, deceiving, could no longer harm.

90. In the middle, not only in the middle of the way

But all the way, in a dark wood, in a bramble,

On the edge of a grimpen, where is no secure foothold,

And menaced by monsters, fancy lights,

東科克
〈四重奏〉之二

安祥只是故意的遲鈍，

80. 智慧只是已死秘密的知識

除非是在他們窺探進去的黑暗中

或是從中他們把眼睛轉開。在我們看來

至多，只是有限的價值

如果知識來自經驗。

85. 知識制約樣式，而且偽造事實，

因為樣式時時刻刻在更新

而且每一時刻是一個新而驚人的、

對我們至今一切的評估。我們只是，在受騙中

從不會再有傷害的迷濛中覺醒。

90. 居於中間，不只是在道的中間

而且是一路上，在暗林中，在荊棘中，

在沒有安全立足點的沼澤邊緣，

而且受到怪獸，幻光的恐嚇，

Risking enchantment. Do not let me hear

95. Of the wisdom of old men, but rather of their folly,

Their fear of fear and frenzy, their fear of possession,

Of belonging to another, or to others, or to God.

The only wisdom we can hope to acquire

Is the wisdom of humility: humility is endless.

100. The houses are all gone under the sea.

The dancers are all gone under the hill.

東科克
〈四重奏〉之二

冒著妖術魅惑的危險。不要讓我聽見

95. 老人的智慧，寧可聽他們的愚行，

他們對恐懼和瘋狂的恐懼，他們對占有的恐懼，

占有屬於另一個人，或別人的，或者上帝的。

我們所能希望獲得的唯一智慧

是謙虛的智慧：謙虛無止境。

100.　　所有的房子都消失在海底下。

　　所有的舞者都消失在山丘下。

East Coker
No.2 of 'Four Quartets'

III

O dark dark dark. They all go into the dark,

The vacant interstellar spaces, the vacant into the vacant,

The captains, merchant bankers, eminent men of letters,

105. The generous patrons of art, the statesmen and the rulers,

Distinguished civil servants, chairmen of many committees,

Industrial lords and petty contractors, all go into the dark,

And dark the Sun and Moon, and the Almanach de Gotha

And the Stock Exchange Gazette, the Directory of Directors,

110. And cold the sense and lost the motive of action.

And we all go with them, into the silent funeral,

Nobody's funeral, for there is no one to bury.

I said to my soul, be still, and let the dark come upon you

Which shall be the darkness of God. As, in a theatre,

東科克
〈四重奏〉之二

III

呵　黑暗黑暗黑暗。一切陷入黑暗

空闊的星際空間，從空缺到空缺

船長，商品銀行家，傑出的文人，

105.　藝術的慷慨恩主，政治家和統治者，

傑出的公僕，委員會的主席諸公，

工業的大咖和小承包商，都陷入黑暗

而日月黯然，以及歐洲皇族家譜

以及股票交易公報，董事名錄

110.　而感知冰冷，失去了行動的動機。

而我們跟他們一起走進沉默的葬禮，

不是誰的葬禮，因為沒有人埋葬。

我對我的靈魂說，稍安勿躁，讓黑暗找上你

那將是上帝的幽闇。有如，在劇院，

East Coker
No.2 of 'Four Quartets'

115. The lights are extinguished, for the scene to be changed

With a hollow rumble of wings, with a movement of darkness

on darkness,

And we know that the hills and the trees, the distant panorama

And the bold imposing facade are all being rolled away—

Or as, when an underground train, in the tube, stops too long

between stations

120. And the conversation rises and slowly fades into silence

And you see behind every face the mental emptiness deepen

Leaving only the growing terror of nothing to think about;

Or when, under ether, the mind is conscious but conscious of

nothing—

I said to my soul, be still, and wait without hope

125. For hope would be hope for the wrong thing; wait without love,

For love would be love of the wrong thing; there is yet faith

東科克
〈四重奏〉之二

115. 燈光熄滅，以便換景

以振翅的空洞聲響，以黑暗疊加黑暗的動作，

而我們知道山崗和樹木，遠處的全景

以及膽大壯觀的正面都會一一被捲走——

或者如，當地下鐵路的列車穿行，在車站之間停留太久

120. 而會話揚起又慢慢消失於沉默

而你在每一張臉後看見精神空虛加深

只留下逐漸滋長的、無話可說的恐懼；

或者，恍惚間，精神雖有意識卻什麼也沒意識到——

我對我的靈魂說，稍安勿躁，等待而不帶希望

125. 因為所希望的會是錯誤的希望；等待而沒有愛

因為所愛的會是錯誤的愛；雖然還有信仰

East Coker
No.2 of 'Four Quartets'

But the faith and the love and the hope are all in the waiting.

Wait without thought, for you are not ready for thought:

So the darkness shall be the light, and the stillness the

dancing.

130.　　Whisper of running streams, and winter lightning.

The wild thyme unseen and the wild strawberry,

The laughter in the garden, echoed ecstasy

Not lost, but requiring, pointing to the agony

Of death and birth.

135.　　　　　　　　　You say I am repeating

Something I have said before. I shall say it again.

Shall I say it again? In order to arrive there,

To arrive where you are, to get from where you are not,

　　You must go by a way wherein there is no ecstasy.

東科克
〈四重奏〉之二

可是信仰、愛和希望都在等待中。

等待而沒有思想,因為你還沒準備好思想;

於是黑暗將成為光,而靜止成為舞姿。

130.　　　溪流的細語,以及冬日的閃電。

看不見的野百里香和野草莓,

花園裡的笑聲,回響的狂喜

不是迷失,而是要求,指向

死與生的苦惱。

135.　　　　　　　你說我一再重複

我以前說過的事。我要再說一次。

我該再說一次?為了到達那兒,

到達你在的地方,從你不在的地方出發,

　　你必須沿著沒有狂喜的一條路。

140. In order to arrive at what you do not know

      You must go by a way which is the way of ignorance.

In order to possess what you do not possess

      You must go by the way of dispossession.

In order to arrive at what you are not

145.   You must go through the way in which you are not.

And what you do not know is the only thing you know

And what you own is what you do not own

And where you are is where you are not.

東科克
〈 四重奏 〉之二

140. 為了到達你所不知道的

　　　你必須沿著一條路、一條無知的路。

　　為了擁有你所沒擁有的

　　　你必須沿著放棄擁有的道路。

　　為了到達你不存在的地方

145. 　　　你必須經過你不存在的道路。

　　而你所不知道的卻是你唯一知道的

　　而你所有的是你所沒有的

　　而你所在的地方是你不在的地方。

East Coker
No.2 of 'Four Quartets'

IV

The wounded surgeon plies the steel
150. That questions the distempered part;
Beneath the bleeding hands we feel
The sharp compassion of the healer's art
Resolving the enigma of the fever chart.

Our only health is the disease
155. If we obey the dying nurse
Whose constant care is not to please
But to remind of our, and Adam's curse,
And that, to be restored, our sickness must grow worse.

The whole earth is our hospital

東科克
〈四重奏〉之二

IV

受傷的外科醫生使用鋼刀

150. 追問有毛病的部位;

在流血的手底下,我們感受到

治癒者的醫術,以銳利的慈愛

解決了體溫表的謎語。

　　我們唯一的健康是疾病

155. 假如我們聽從臨死護士的話

她的加護照顧不是為了安慰我們

而是提醒我們,亞當的詛咒,

甚至為了恢復,我們的病情必須更加惡化。

　　整個地球是我們的醫院

East Coker

160. Endowed by the ruined millionaire,

Wherein, if we do well, we shall

Die of the absolute paternal care

That will not leave us, but prevents us everywhere.

The chill ascends from feet to knees,

165. The fever sings in mental wires.

If to be warmed, then I must freeze

And quake in frigid purgatorial fires

Of which the flame is roses, and the smoke is briars.

The dripping blood our only drink,

170. The bloody flesh our only food:

In spite of which we like to think

That we are sound, substantial flesh and blood—

Again, in spite of that, we call this Friday good.

東科克
〈四重奏〉之二

160. 得到破產的百萬富人的捐贈

在這醫院裡，假如一切順利，我們將會

為照顧不顧一切的父親而死去

因他絕不離棄我們，而是到處保護我們。

　　　惡寒從腳底上升到膝蓋，

165. 發燒在腦髓的鐵線中歌唱。

為了取暖，那麼我必須凍僵

在嚴寒的煉獄火中顫抖，

那火焰是野玫瑰，煙是荊棘。

　　　滴淌的血是我們唯一的飲料，

170. 沾血的肉是我們唯一的食物：

儘管如此，我們寧可認為

我們是健全而有實質的血肉之軀——

而且，儘管如此，我們認為這是耶穌受難的聖週五。

V

So here I am, in the middle way, having had twenty years—

175. Twenty years largely wasted, the years of l'entre deux guerres

Trying to use words, and every attempt

Is a wholly new start, and a different kind of failure

Because one has only learnt to get the better of words

For the thing one no longer has to say, or the way in which

180. One is no longer disposed to say it. And so each venture

Is a new beginning, a raid on the inarticulate

With shabby equipment always deteriorating

In the general mess of imprecision of feeling,

Undisciplined squads of emotion. And what there is to

conquer

185. By strength and submission, has already been discovered

東科克
〈四重奏〉之二

V

於是我在這裡，在中間，已有二十年——

175. 大多浪費的二十年，在兩次戰爭之間的歲月

每次企圖使用語言

都是全新的開始，不一樣的失敗

因為人們剛學到較會使用語言時

卻發現要說的已不需要說了，

180. 或者已不是準備要說的。因此每一次冒險

都是新的開始，對不善辭令的攻擊

卻以一再退步的簡陋裝備

陷入感情無法準確表達的一般混亂中

未經訓練的情緒的小部隊。

185. 況且需要以強勢和順從征服的，已被發現，一再地甚至好

幾次，正是

Once or twice, or several times, by men whom one cannot hope

To emulate—but there is no competition—

There is only the fight to recover what has been lost

And found and lost again and again: and now, under conditions

190. That seem unpropitious. But perhaps neither gain nor loss.

For us, there is only the trying. The rest is not our business.

Home is where one starts from. As we grow older

The world becomes stranger, the pattern more complicated

Of dead and living. Not the intense moment

195. Isolated, with no before and after,

But a lifetime burning in every moment

And not the lifetime of one man only

東科克
〈四重奏〉之二

人們不能寄望

對抗——可是沒有競爭——的那些人。

只有奮力恢復一再失去

而又找到的東西：而當今似乎處於

190. 不吉利的情勢。但也許無關得失。

對我們，只有盡力而為。其餘的不關我們的事。

家是一個人出發的地方。隨著年歲增加

世界越來越疏遠，而生與死的樣式

更加複雜。沒有緊張的時刻

195. 孤零零的，沒有過去也沒有未來

而是一生時時刻刻都在燃燒

而且不只是一個人的一生

East Coker
No.2 of 'Four Quartets'

But of old stones that cannot be deciphered.

There is a time for the evening under starlight,

200. A time for the evening under lamplight

(The evening with the photograph album).

Love is most nearly itself

When here and now cease to matter

Old men ought to be explorers

205. Here or there does not matter

We must be still and still moving

Into another intensity

For a further union, a deeper communion

Through the dark cold and the empty desolation,

210. The wave cry, the wind cry, the vast waters

Of the petrel and the porpoise. In my end is my beginning.

東科克
〈四重奏〉之二

而是難以解讀的古代石碑的一生。

既有星光下夜晚的時刻

200. 也有燈光下夜晚的時刻

（照相簿的夜晚）。

愛最接近它本身

一旦此時此地不再是問題。

老人應該是探險者

205. 這裡或那裡不是問題

我們必須靜止而靜止移動

進入另一緊張

為了進一步的融合，更深的靈契

透過黑暗寒冷和空虛的孤寂，

210. 浪在喊叫，風在喊叫，海燕和海豚的

無涯海原。我的結束就是我的開始。

East Coker
No.2 of 'Four Quartets'

---

1 譯註：東科克（East Coker）是位於英國英格蘭西南部的薩默塞特郡
（Somerset）的一個鄉村，北臨布里斯托灣。

· No.3 ·

The Dry Salvages[1]

岬岸礁岩

〈 四重奏 〉之三

The Dry Salvages
No.3 of 'Four Quartets'

I

I do not know much about gods; but I think that the river

Is a strong brown god—sullen, untamed and intractable,

Patient to some degree, at first recognised as a frontier;

Useful, untrustworthy, as a conveyor of commerce;

5. Then only a problem confronting the builder of bridges.

The problem once solved, the brown god is almost forgotten

By the dwellers in cities—ever, however, implacable.

Keeping his seasons and rages, destroyer, reminder

Of what men choose to forget. Unhonoured, unpropitiated

10. By worshippers of the machine, but waiting, watching and

waiting.

His rhythm was present in the nursery bedroom,

In the rank ailanthus of the April dooryard,

岬岸礁岩
〈四重奏〉之三

I

我對異神所知不多；但我認為河流

是一個強大的褐色的神——繃著臉，倔強不馴，難以對付的，

有幾分的耐性，最初被認為是一個開疆者；

有用的，不值得信任的，像商業的運送者；

5. 後來只是造橋者所面臨的一個問題。

問題一旦解決，褐色的神就幾乎

讓城市的居民給遺忘了——可是永遠記恨在心。

忘不了自己的季節和憤怒，一個破壞者，

提醒人們寧願忘卻的事情。未受機器崇拜者的尊崇，

10. 得不到慰藉，只是等待，眼睜睜地等待。

河流的節奏存在於幼兒的臥室

於四月前庭繁茂的椿樹，

In the smell of grapes on the autumn table,

And the evening circle in the winter gaslight.

15.   The river is within us, the sea is all about us;

The sea is the land's edge also, the granite

Into which it reaches, the beaches where it tosses

Its hints of earlier and other creation:

The starfish, the horseshoe crab, the whale's backbone;

20. The pools where it offers to our curiosity

The more delicate algae and the sea anemone.

It tosses up our losses, the torn seine,

The shattered lobsterpot, the broken oar

And the gear of foreign dead men. The sea has many voices,

25. Many gods and many voices.

岬岸礁岩
〈四重奏〉之三

於秋日餐桌上葡萄的氣味，

以及冬季瓦斯燈下的晚會。

15.　　　河流在我們體內，海包圍著我們；

海也是陸地的邊沿，

海所滲透的花崗岩，它在海灘拋擲

令人聯想到創世及其他創造物：

海星，馬蹄蟹，鯨魚的背骨；

20.　水塘提供給我們的好奇心

更微妙的藻類以及海葵。

海翻起我們失去的東西，扯破的大漁網，

破碎的捕蝦簍，斷折的划槳

以及死了的外地人的衣物。海有許多聲音，

25.　許多神和許多聲音。

The Dry Salvages
No.3 of 'Four Quartets'

The salt is on the briar rose,

The fog is in the fir trees.

The sea howl

And the sea yelp, are different voices

30. Often together heard: the whine in the rigging,

The menace and caress of wave that breaks on water,

The distant rote in the granite teeth,

And the wailing warning from the approaching headland

Are all sea voices, and the heaving groaner

35. Rounded homewards, and the seagull:

And under the oppression of the silent fog

The tolling bell

Measures time not our time, rung by the unhurried

Ground swell, a time

40. Older than the time of chronometers, older

岬岸礁岩
〈四重奏〉之三

鹽在荊棘的玫瑰上，

霧氣在樅樹林間。

海的嚎哮

以及海的叫喊，是不同的聲音

30. 常常聽起來混在一起：索具的哀鳴

破浪在海上激起的威嚇和愛撫

在遠方一再拍打花崗岩牙齒的浪濤，

以及接近陸岬發出警告的哀號

這些都是海的聲音，而起伏的吹鳴浮標

35. 轉向家鄉，以及海鷗：

以及在靜默的霧氣壓迫下

悠揚的鐘聲

計量時間，那不是我們的時間；

海底捲起的巨浪緩緩移動，它所敲響的時間，

40. 比計時器的時間更古老

The Dry Salvages
No.3 of 'Four Quartets'

Than time counted by anxious worried women

Lying awake, calculating the future,

Trying to unweave, unwind, unravel

And piece together the past and the future,

45. Between midnight and dawn, when the past is all deception,

The future futureless, before the morning watch

When time stops and time is never ending;

And the ground swell, that is and was from the beginning,

Clangs

50. The bell.

岬岸礁岩
〈四重奏〉之三

比憂心如焚的女人所思量的時間更古老

當她清醒地躺在床上，計算未來，

盡力想要拆織，捲回，解開

而將過去和未來串在一起，

45. 在午夜和黎明之間，當過去盡是欺騙，

而未來沒有未來，在凌晨守望之前

當時間停止而時間永無了時；

而滔天巨浪，從一開始而且曾經，

鏗然敲響

50. 鐘聲。

II

Where is there an end of it, the soundless wailing,

The silent withering of autumn flowers

Dropping their petals and remaining motionless;

Where is there an end to the drifting wreckage,

55.   The prayer of the bone on the beach, the unprayable

Prayer at the calamitous annunciation?

    There is no end, but addition: the trailing

Consequence of further days and hours,

While emotion takes to itself the emotionless

60.   Years of living among the breakage

Of what was believed in as the most reliable—

And therefore the fittest for renunciation.

岬岸礁岩

〈四重奏〉之三

II

不幸何時才是終了，無聲的悲嘆，

秋天的花默默凋萎

落下花瓣而且靜止不動；

船難的殘骸最後漂流何處，

55.　沙灘上白骨的禱告，無以禱告的

禱告，面對著不幸災厄的聞報？

　　　沒有終了，反而追加：拖著

隨後日月和時間的尾巴，

當感動自身成為毫無感動

60.　而生活在歲月的殘片中

那些曾被相信是最為可靠的歲月——

因此宣布放棄是最適當的。

The Dry Salvages
No.3 of 'Four Quartets'

There is the final addition, the failing

Pride or resentment at failing powers,

65. The unattached devotion which might pass for devotionless,

In a drifting boat with a slow leakage,

The silent listening to the undeniable

Clamour of the bell of the last annunciation.

Where is the end of them, the fishermen sailing

70. Into the wind's tail, where the fog cowers?

We cannot think of a time that is oceanless

Or of an ocean not littered with wastage

Or of a future that is not liable

Like the past, to have no destination.

岬岸礁岩
〈四重奏〉之三

　　最後追加一句，逐漸失去的
自豪或是對權力逐漸失去的憤慨，
65.　沒有熱忱的信仰可能被當作沒有信仰，
在慢慢漏水的漂流小船上，
默默靜聽無可否認的
宣告：最後聞報的鐘聲。

　　這些何時終了，漁夫把船
70.　駛入霧氣畏縮的風尾？
我們無法想像沒有海洋的時候
或是垃圾凌亂的海洋
或是不可靠的未來
一如沒有目的地的過去。

The Dry Salvages
No.3 of 'Four Quartets'

75.   We have to think of them as forever bailing,

Setting and hauling, while the North East lowers

Over shallow banks unchanging and erosionless

Or drawing their money, drying sails at dockage;

Not as making a trip that will be unpayable

80.   For a haul that will not bear examination.

There is no end of it, the voiceless wailing,

No end to the withering of withered flowers,

To the movement of pain that is painless and motionless,

To the drift of the sea and the drifting wreckage,

85.   The bone's prayer to Death its God. Only the hardly, barely

prayable

Prayer of the one Annunciation.

岬岸礁岩
〈四重奏〉之三

75.　　　我們必須想到漁夫們經常在排水

張帆，拖網，當東北季風低吹過

保持不變而且不受侵蝕的淺灘

或者去提款，在碼頭晾乾船帆；

不至於出海一趟，而結果因漁獲

80.　沒通過檢查而得不到付款。

　　　沒有終了的時候，而無聲的哀嘆，

凋謝的花朵，凋謝無時終了，

無痛感而一動不動的痛苦的動作無時終了，

海的漂流以及漂流的殘骸無時終了，

85.　白骨向死亡的主宰的禱告。只有幾幾乎無法禱告的

唯一「聞報」的禱告。

It seems, as one becomes older,

That the past has another pattern, and ceases to be a mere sequence—

Or even development: the latter a partial fallacy

90. Encouraged by superficial notions of evolution,

Which becomes, in the popular mind, a means of disowning the past.

The moments of happiness—not the sense of well-being,

Fruition, fulfilment, security or affection,

Or even a very good dinner, but the sudden illumination—

95. We had the experience but missed the meaning,

And approach to the meaning restores the experience

In a different form, beyond any meaning

We can assign to happiness. I have said before

That the past experience revived in the meaning

100. Is not the experience of one life only

But of many generations—not forgetting

岬岸礁岩
〈四重奏〉之三

隨著年紀的增長，似乎

過去有了另一模式，不再僅僅是連續——

甚至也不是進展：後者是一種偏頗的謬論

90. 受到進化論膚淺觀念的鼓勵，

而在一般人的心中，成為否認過去的手段。

幸福的時刻——不是指樂活，

成果，實現，安心或摯愛的感覺，

或甚至是一頓很好的晚餐，而是指突然的啟示亦即頓悟——

95. 我們有這經驗但不了解意義，

而接近意義意味著回復過去的經驗

以不同的形式，超過我們所能

給予幸福的任何意義。我以前說過

過去的經驗在意義中復活

100. 這不只是一個人一生的經驗

而是許多世代的經驗——遺忘不了

Something that is probably quite ineffable:

The backward look behind the assurance

Of recorded history, the backward half-look

105. Over the shoulder, towards the primitive terror.

Now, we come to discover that the moments of agony

(Whether, or not, due to misunderstanding,

Having hoped for the wrong things or dreaded the wrong things,

Is not in question) are likewise permanent

110. With such permanence as time has. We appreciate this better

In the agony of others, nearly experienced,

Involving ourselves, than in our own.

For our own past is covered by the currents of action,

But the torment of others remains an experience

115. Unqualified, unworn by subsequent attrition.

People change, and smile: but the agony abides.

岬岸礁岩
〈四重奏〉之三

可能很難表達的某種東西：

以回顧的眼光，看看歷史記載的保證背後，

從肩膀上，側目回顧

105. 看看那原始的恐怖。

這時，我們開始發現，苦惱的瞬間

（不論是否由於誤解，問題不在於

對錯誤事情抱持希望或害怕錯誤的事情），

也是永恆的，與時間那種永恆是一樣的。

110. 我們更能體會這點

當我們處在別人的苦惱中，幾乎體驗到

感同身受，甚於對我們自身的苦惱。

因為我們本身的過去受到行動潮流的矇蔽，

而對別人的折騰依然只是一種

115. 無條件的經驗，不因後來的悔罪而有所磨損。

人們改變，微笑著：可是苦惱持續不變。

Time the destroyer is time the preserver,

Like the river with its cargo of dead negroes, cows and chicken coops,

The bitter apple, and the bite in the apple.

120. And the ragged rock in the restless waters,

Waves wash over it, fogs conceal it;

On a halcyon day it is merely a monument,

In navigable weather it is always a seamark

To lay a course by: but in the sombre season

125. Or the sudden fury, is what it always was.

岬岸礁岩
〈四重奏〉之三

時間是破壞者，時間也是保存者，

就像河上的貨船，運載死去的黑人，母牛和鷄籠，

苦蘋果，以及蘋果的咬痕，

120.　不寧的海上凹凸不平的岩石，

受波浪沖洗，霧氣籠罩；

風平浪靜的時日它只是一個紀念碑，

天氣可以出航時，它經常是

引導航線的標識：可是在晦暗季節

125.　或是突起的狂濤中，岩石仍像往昔一樣。

The Dry Salvages
No.3 of 'Four Quartets'

III

I sometimes wonder if that is what Krishna meant—

Among other things—or one way of putting the same thing:

That the future is a faded song, a Royal Rose or a lavender

spray

Of wistful regret for those who are not yet here to regret,

130. Pressed between yellow leaves of a book that has never been

opened.

And the way up is the way down, the way forward is the way

back.

You cannot face it steadily, but this thing is sure,

That time is no healer: the patient is no longer here.

When the train starts, and the passengers are settled

135. To fruit, periodicals and business letters

岬岸礁岩
〈四重奏〉之三

III

我有時候在想，那是否克利西納的本意——

其中，或許是藉以表達同樣意思的一種說法：

未來是一首消逝了的歌，一朵皇室玫瑰或者一根薰衣草

花枝

帶著憂傷的後悔，對那些還沒出生來表示後悔的人，

130. 被壓在從來沒打開的一本書發黃的書頁間。

而且上行道就是下行道，前頭路就是回頭路。

你無法堅定地面對它，但這事是真的，

時間不是治癒者：病人已經不在人間。

當列車開動，而旅客安頓下來

135. 吃水果，看報刊，處理商務信件，

(And those who saw them off have left the platform)

Their faces relax from grief into relief,

To the sleepy rhythm of a hundred hours.

Fare forward, travellers! not escaping from the past

140. Into different lives, or into any future;

You are not the same people who left that station

Or who will arrive at any terminus,

While the narrowing rails slide together behind you;

And on the deck of the drumming liner

145. Watching the furrow that widens behind you,

You shall not think 'the past is finished'

Or 'the future is before us'.

At nightfall, in the rigging and the aerial,

Is a voice descanting (though not to the ear,

150. The murmuring shell of time, and not in any language)

岬岸礁岩
〈四重奏〉之三

（這些送行的人都已離開月台）

他們的臉，從悲傷變成輕鬆，

應和著一百小時的節奏的催眠。

旅人喲，往前走！不要逃避過去

140.　逃到不同的人生，或者未來；

你與離開那車站

或者將到達任何終點的那些人不同

當你背後越來越窄的軌道滑成一道；

而在鼓聲震響的郵輪甲板上

145.　望著航跡在你背後越來越擴大

你不要認為「過去已經結束」

或是「未來前程在望」。

夜來，在索具和天線中

有一種聲音在歌唱（雖然不是對著耳朵，

150.　喃喃不斷的時間的貝殼，也不是任何語言）

The Dry Salvages
No.3 of 'Four Quartets'

'Fare forward, you who think that you are voyaging;

You are not those who saw the harbor

Receding, or those who will disembark.

Here between the hither and the farther shore

155. While time is withdrawn, consider the future

And the past with an equal mind.

At the moment which is not of action or inaction

You can receive this: "on whatever sphere of being

The mind of a man may be intent

160. At the time of death"—that is the one action

(And the time of death is every moment)

Which shall fructify in the lives of others:

And do not think of the fruit of action.

Fare forward.

165.   O voyagers, O seamen,

岬岸礁岩
〈四重奏〉之三

「往前走吧，自認為是遠航的旅人們；

你們不是那些眺望著港口

逐漸遠去的人，也不是那些要下船的人。

如今在此地和此後的岸上之間

155. 當抽出時間的時候，以相等的心情

考慮未來和過去吧。

在既不是作為也不是無作為的瞬間

你可以接受這點：『臨死時一個人的繫心之念

不論是在於哪種存在領域』——

160. 這種執念是一種作為

（而死的瞬間是時時刻刻的）

導致在別人的生命中結了果：

然則不要考慮這種作為的結果。

往前走吧。

165. 　　　　　遠航的旅人喲，航海者喲，

The Dry Salvages
No.3 of 'Four Quartets'

You who came to port, and you whose bodies

Will suffer the trial and judgement of the sea,

Or whatever event, this is your real destination.'

So Krishna, as when he admonished Arjuna

170. On the field of battle

Not fare well,

But fare forward, voyagers.

岬岸礁岩
〈四重奏〉之三

來到港口的你們，身體

將接受海的審判和判決的你們，

不論如何，這是你們真正的目的地。」

因此，一如克利西納在戰場上

170. 對亞吉納的告誡所說的。

                  不是告別，

還是往前走吧，遠航的旅人。

IV

Lady, whose shrine stands on the promontory,

Pray for all those who are in ships, those

175. Whose business has to do with fish, and

Those concerned with every lawful traffic

And those who conduct them.

  Repeat a prayer also on behalf of

Women who have seen their sons or husbands

180. Setting forth, and not returning:

Figlia del tuo figlio,

Queen of Heaven.

  Also pray for those who were in ships, and

岬岸礁岩
〈四重奏〉之三

IV

聖母喲，您的神殿聳立在岬角上，

為所有乘船的人們禱告，那些

175. 從事漁業的人，以及

那些與每一合法貿易有關的人

還有那些指導他們的人。

請一再禱告，也為那些女人

她們看著兒子和丈夫出發

180. 卻不見他們回來：

汝子的女兒，

天上的王后喲。

也為在船上的那些人禱告，

The Dry Salvages
No.3 of 'Four Quartets'

Ended their voyage on the sand, in the sea's lips

185. Or in the dark throat which will not reject them

Or wherever cannot reach them the sound of the sea bell's

Perpetual angelus.

岬岸礁岩
〈四重奏〉之三

　　而他們的航行終於觸礁，流入海的口唇

185.　或者黑暗的喉嚨不把他們吐出來

　　或在海的鐘聲，永恆的祈禱鐘

　　傳不到他們的任何地方。

V

To communicate with Mars, converse with spirits,

To report the behaviour of the sea monster,

190. Describe the horoscope, haruspicate or scry,

Observe disease in signatures, evoke

Biography from the wrinkles of the palm

And tragedy from fingers; release omens

By sortilege, or tea leaves, riddle the inevitable

195. With playing cards, fiddle with pentagrams

Or barbituric acids, or dissect

The recurrent image into pre-conscious terrors—

To explore the womb, or tomb, or dreams; all these are usual

Pastimes and drugs, and features of the press:

200. And always will be, some of them especially

岬岸礁岩
〈四重奏〉之三

V

與火星通訊，與神靈對話，

報導海怪的行為，

190. 描述占星術、臟占或水晶占，

署名觀察病狀，從手掌的皺紋

喚起一生的傳記，

從手指看出悲劇；以抽籤

或茶葉斷言吉凶，

195. 以撲克牌解謎注定的命運，以五芒星形

或是巴比妥酸玩弄手法，或者剖析

重複出現的心象而歸於意識以前的恐怖──

探究子宮、墳墓，或者夢；這些都是

普通的娛樂和麻藥，以及新聞特稿：

200. 這些將永遠如此，其中有些特別是，

The Dry Salvages
No.3 of 'Four Quartets'

When there is distress of nations and perplexity

Whether on the shores of Asia, or in the Edgware Road.

Men's curiosity searches past and future

And clings to that dimension. But to apprehend

205. The point of intersection of the timeless

With time, is an occupation for the saint—

No occupation either, but something given

And taken, in a lifetime's death in love,

Ardour and selflessness and self-surrender.

210. For most of us, there is only the unattended

Moment, the moment in and out of time,

The distraction fit, lost in a shaft of sunlight,

The wild thyme unseen, or the winter lightning

Or the waterfall, or music heard so deeply

215. That it is not heard at all, but you are the music

岬岸礁岩
〈四重奏〉之三

當民族災難和困境發生時

不論是在亞洲沿岸，或在倫敦的埃奇威爾路。

人類的好奇心探索過去和未來

而且固執在那一次元。但是領會

205. 無限時間與時間的交叉點，

是聖者的一個職業——

不是職業，而是某種有給有得的交易

一生至死，對愛、

熱誠、無私和無我的奉獻。

210. 對大部分的我們，只有未被關注的

瞬間，在時間之中和之外的瞬間，

迷失在太陽的光芒中，恍神的發作

看不見的野百里香，或者冬日的閃電

或者瀑布，或者音樂，聽得如此沉醉

215. 你完全沒聽到，但是只要音樂繼續

While the music lasts. These are only hints and guesses,

Hints followed by guesses; and the rest

Is prayer, observance, discipline, thought and action.

The hint half guessed, the gift half understood, is Incarnation.

220. Here the impossible union

Of spheres of existence is actual,

Here the past and future

Are conquered, and reconciled,

Where action were otherwise movement

225. Of that which is only moved

And has in it no source of movement—

Driven by daemonic, chthonic

Powers. And right action is freedom

From past and future also.

230. For most of us, this is the aim

岬岸礁岩
〈四重奏〉之三

你就變成那音樂。這些都只是暗示和猜想，

暗示跟隨著猜想；而其餘的是

禱告，戒律，苦行，冥想和行動。

一半猜想的暗示，一半領悟的天賦，這是神的權化。

220. 於此，兩種存在領域的

不可能的結合實現了，

於此，過去和未來

被克服，而且和解，

否則行動只是

225. 被移動的運動

當中沒有運動的原動力——

只是受到惡魔和地獄力的驅使。

正當的行動是自由

不受過去也不受未來的拘束。

230. 對於大部分的我們，這是

Never here to be realised;

Who are only undefeated

Because we have gone on trying;

We, content at the last

235. If our temporal reversion nourish

(Not too far from the yew-tree)

The life of significant soil.

岬岸礁岩
〈四重奏〉之三

在這世上未曾實現的目標;

我們立於不敗之地

只因我們至今一再努力;

我們,最後該會瞑目

235. 假如我們的現世生命返回先祖

（距離紫杉樹不太遠）

能夠滋養意義深遠的土地的生命。

原註

1. 「The Dry Salvages」該是「les trois sauvages」（三個野蠻人）的
   訛傳，是指一小群的岩礁，上有信標燈塔，在麻薩諸塞州東北角安妮海
   岬的岸邊。「Salvages」的發音與「assuages」叶韻。Groaner（呻
   吟者）：指吹鳴的浮標。

Little Gidding

小吉丁[1]

〈四重奏〉之四

Little Gidding
No.4 of 'Four Quartets'

I

Midwinter spring is its own season

Sempiternal though sodden towards sundown,

Suspended in time, between pole and tropic.

When the short day is brightest, with frost and fire,

5. The brief sun flames the ice, on pond and ditches,

In windless cold that is the heart's heat,

Reflecting in a watery mirror

A glare that is blindness in the early afternoon.

And glow more intense than blaze of branch, or brazier,

10. Stirs the dumb spirit: no wind, but pentecostal fire

In the dark time of the year. Between melting and freezing

The soul's sap quivers. There is no earth smell

Or smell of living thing. This is the spring time

小吉丁
〈四重奏〉之四

I

仲冬的春天自成一個季節

是永遠的雖然近日落時濕淋淋，

時間停頓在極地與熱帶之間。

當短短的一日，因霜與火，最為明亮的時候，

5. 短暫的太陽在池塘和溝渠上點燃冰，

在無風的寒冷亦即心的熱火中，

從水鏡中反射出

午後盲目刺眼的亮光。

而且比燃燒的樹枝或火缽更強烈的輝光

10. 騷動喑啞的靈魂：無風，只有聖靈降臨節的火

照亮年中這一黑暗的季節。在溶化和凍結之間

靈魂的樹液在顫動。沒有泥土的氣息

或是生物的氣息。這是春的季節

Little Gidding
No.4 of 'Four Quartets'

But not in time's covenant. Now the hedgerow

15. Is blanched for an hour with transitory blossom

Of snow, a bloom more sudden

Than that of summer, neither budding nor fading,

Not in the scheme of generation.

Where is the summer, the unimaginable

20. Zero summer?

If you came this way,

Taking the route you would be likely to take

From the place you would be likely to come from,

If you came this way in may time, you would find the hedges

25. White again, in May, with voluptuary sweetness.

It would be the same at the end of the journey,

If you came at night like a broken king,

小吉丁
〈四重奏〉之四

但不在時間的約定中。此時樹籬

15. 因無常的雪花一時變白，

比夏天的花季更突然的

盛開，不是萌芽也不是凋謝，

不在生育的結構中。

夏天在哪兒，難以想像的

20. 零夏天？

假如你從這條路來

走你可能會走的道路

從你可能會來的地方來，

假如你在山楂子盛開時節從這條路走來，你會發現樹籬

25. 又都變白了，在五月，帶著官能的美。

那會是一樣的，到了旅途的終點，

假如你晚上來像一個落魄的國王，

If you came by day not knowing what you came for,

It would be the same, when you leave the rough road

30. And turn behind the pig-sty to the dull façade

And the tombstone. And what you thought you came for

Is only a shell, a husk of meaning

From which the purpose breaks only when it is fulfilled

If at all. Either you had no purpose

35. Or the purpose is beyond the end you figured

And is altered in fulfilment. There are other places

Which also are the world's end, some at the sea jaws,

Which also are the world's end, some at the sea jaws,

But this is the nearest, in place and time,

40. Now and in England.

If you came this way,

小吉丁
〈 四重奏 〉之四

假如你白天來不知道你為什麼來，

那會是一樣的，當你離開崎嶇不平的路

30. 繞到豬圈後面走向無趣的建築正面

以及墓碑。而且你以為你來的目的

只是為了一個貝殼，一個意義的外萊，

從中，意圖必然落空一旦獲得滿足，

如果真的獲得滿足。你若不是沒有意圖

35. 就是你的意圖是在心中的目的之外，

而在滿足中已經改變。有些其他地方

也是世界的終點，有的在海的顎口，

或在越過陰暗湖面的地方，在沙漠或城市——

可是在地點和時間上，最接近的是

40. 此時，在英格蘭。

假如你從這條路來，

Little Gidding
No.4 of 'Four Quartets'

Taking any route, starting from anywhere,

At any time or at any season,

It would always be the same: you would have to put off

45.   Sense and notion. You are not here to verify,

Instruct yourself, or inform curiosity

Or carry report. You are here to kneel

Where prayer has been valid. And prayer is more

Than an order of words, the conscious occupation

50.   Of the praying mind, or the sound of the voice praying.

And what the dead had no speech for, when living,

They can tell you, being dead: the communication

Of the dead is tongued with fire beyond the language of the

living.

Here, the intersection of the timeless moment

55.   Is England and nowhere. Never and always.

小吉丁
〈四重奏〉之四

走任何一條路,從任何地方出發

在任何時候或任何季節,

那會都是一樣的:你會不得不丟棄

45. 感覺和觀念。你來這兒不是為了證明事實,

訓導自己,告知好奇心

或進行報導。你來這兒是為了跪下

這是祈禱一向應驗的地方。而且禱告不限於

字句的次序,自覺的

50. 祈禱心的專注,或者禱告的聲音。

而死者,在世時,無法用語言表達的,

他們能告訴你,就是死:死者的傳達

是以火的舌頭,超越活者的語言。

這裡,永恆瞬間的交叉點,

55. 是英格蘭而不是任何地方。永遠不是而且始終不是。

Little Gidding
No.4 of 'Four Quartets'

II

Ash on an old man's sleeve

Is all the ash the burnt roses leave.

Dust in the air suspended

Marks the place where a story ended.

60. Dust inbreathed was a house—

The walls, the wainscot and the mouse,

The death of hope and despair,

    This is the death of air.

    There are flood and drouth

65. Over the eyes and in the mouth,

Dead water and dead sand

Contending for the upper hand.

小吉丁
〈四重奏〉之四

II

一個老人袖子上的灰

都是焚燒的玫瑰留下的灰。

浮懸在空中的灰塵

標示一個故事結束的地方。

60. 吸進去的灰塵曾是住屋——

牆壁、壁板和老鼠,

希望和絕望的死,

      這是大氣的死。

有洪水和旱災

65. 在眼上,在口中,

死的水和死的沙

互爭看誰居上風。

Little Gidding
No.4 of 'Four Quartets'

The parched eviscerate soil

Gapes at the vanity of toil,

70.   Laughs without mirth,

      This is the death of earth.

   Water and fire succeed

The town, the pasture and the weed.

Water and fire deride

75.   The sacrifice that we denied

Water and fire shall rot

The marred foundations we forgot,

Of sanctuary and choir.

      This is the death of water and fire.

80.   In the uncertain hour before the morning

小吉丁

〈四重奏〉之四

剔骨除腸的乾枯土壤

對著徒勞的虛榮目瞪口呆,

70.　沒有歡笑的笑,

　　　　這是土地的死。

　　　水和火跟隨著

城鄉、牧場和雜草。

水和火嘲笑

75.　我們所否定的犧牲。

水和火將腐蝕

我們所遺忘被汙損的基礎,

聖堂和唱詩班席位。

　　　　這是水和火的死。

80.　　在天亮之前的未確定時刻

Little Gidding
No.4 of 'Four Quartets'

Near the ending of interminable night

At the recurrent end of the unending

After the dark dove with the flickering tongue

Had passed below the horizon of his homing

85. While the dead leaves still rattled on like tin

Over the asphalt where no other sound was

Between three districts whence the smoke arose

I met one walking, loitering and hurried

As if blown towards me like the metal leaves

90. Before the urban dawn wind unresisting.

And as I fixed upon the down-turned face

That pointed scrutiny with which we challenge

The first-met stranger in the waning dusk

I caught the sudden look of some dead master

95. Whom I had known, forgotten, half recalled

小吉丁

〈四重奏〉之四

接近無底洞夜晚的盡頭

在無止盡重複出現的盡頭

在暗黑的鴿子閃現出舌頭

飛過回家的水平線下之後,

85.　枯葉仍在嘎嘎作響如錫罐

滾過別無聲音的柏油路,

在冒起煙的三個地區之間,

我遇見一個在遊蕩而腳步匆匆的人,

似乎被吹向我,有如金屬葉片

90.　在無法抵抗的都市黎明的風前。

當我凝視著朝下的臉

我們挑戰以尖銳眼光仔細檢視

在逐漸褪去的暮色中初次見到的陌生人,

我突然看到某位已故的大師

95.　我曾經認識,忘記了,一半想起,

Little Gidding
No.4 of 'Four Quartets'

Both one and many; in the brown baked features

The eyes of a familiar compound ghost

Both intimate and unidentifiable.

So I assumed a double part, and cried

100.   And heard another's voice cry: 'What! are you here?'

Although we were not. I was still the same,

Knowing myself yet being someone other—

And he a face still forming; yet the words sufficed

To compel the recognition they preceded.

105.   And so, compliant to the common wind,

Too strange to each other for misunderstanding,

In concord at this intersection time

Of meeting nowhere, no before and after,

We trod the pavement in a dead patrol.

110.   I said: 'The wonder that I feel is easy,

小吉丁
〈四重奏〉之四

　　同時是一個也是多個；在曬成褐色的面貌中

　　一個熟悉的複合幽靈的眼睛

既親近又無法確認。

　　於是我承擔兩個角色，呼叫

100.　而聽到另一個叫聲：「怎麼！你在這兒？」

雖然我們不是。我還是我，

　　知道我自己還是另外的一個人——

　　而他，一個還在成形的臉；然而這些對話足以

勉強當作打招呼，表示彼此認識。

105.　於是，順從共同的風向，

　　彼此太陌生就不會產生誤解，

協和一致，在這交叉的時刻

　　不在哪兒見過面，不在過去也不在未來，

　　我們在鋪道上，走出死的巡邏。

110.　我說：「我對驚奇的感覺是安易，

Little Gidding
No.4 of 'Four Quartets'

Yet ease is cause of wonder. Therefore speak:

I may not comprehend, may not remember.'

And he: 'I am not eager to rehearse

My thoughts and theory which you have forgotten.

115.   These things have served their purpose: let them be.

So with your own, and pray they be forgiven

By others, as I pray you to forgive

Both bad and good. Last season's fruit is eaten

And the fullfed beast shall kick the empty pail.

120.   For last year's words belong to last year's language

And next year's words await another voice

But, as the passage now presents no hindrance

To the spirit unappeased and peregrine

Between two worlds become much like each other,

125.   So I find words I never thought to speak

小吉丁
〈四重奏〉之四

然而安易是驚奇的原因。因此請說吧：

我可能不了解，也可能記不住。」

他說：「我不太想複誦

我的思想和理論，那些你都已經忘了，

115.　這些事已達到了目的；就算了吧。

因此對你自己的事，就祈求別人把它忘掉吧，

正像我祈求你的寬恕，

不論是好是壞。上一季節的水果已經吃了

而餵飽了的動物將踢開空水桶。

120.　因為去年的字句屬於去年的語言

而明年的字句等待另一種聲音。

可是，現在由於在越來越相似的

兩個世界之間游移不寧的

精神通道沒有呈現出阻礙，

125.　因此我發現了我從來沒想過要說的話，

Little Gidding
No.4 of 'Four Quartets'

In streets I never thought I should revisit

When I left my body on a distant shore.

Since our concern was speech, and speech impelled us

To purify the dialect of the tribe

130. And urge the mind to aftersight and foresight,

Let me disclose the gifts reserved for age

To set a crown upon your lifetime's effort

First, the cold friction of expiring sense

Without enchantment, offering no promise

135. But bitter tastelessness of shadow fruit

As body and soul begin to fall asunder.

Second, the conscious impotence of rage

At human folly, and the laceration

Of laughter at what ceases to amuse.

140. And last, the rending pain of re-enactment

小吉丁
〈四重奏〉之四

在我從來沒想過再去的街道

當我已把我的身體留在遙遠的岸邊。

既然我們關切的是言語，而言語驅使我們

淨化部族的方言

130.　而促使心靈去反觀和預見，

讓我披露保存給老年的賜物，

為你終生的努力戴上皇冠。

首先，逐漸失去知覺的冷冷摩擦

毫無迷惑，沒有期待

135.　只有幽靈水果苦澀的無味感，

當肉體和靈魂開始分裂的時候。

其次，對人類的愚行感到憤怒的

自覺無力感，以及

對不再有樂趣的事物的苦笑。

140.　最後，一再重演的傷痛，

Little Gidding
No.4 of 'Four Quartets'

Of all that you have done, and been; the shame

Of motives late revealed, and the awareness

Of things ill done and done to others' harm

Which once you took for exercise of virtue

145. Then fools' approval stings, and honour stains.

From wrong to wrong the exasperated spirit

Proceeds, unless restored by that refining fire

Where you must move in measure, like a dancer.'

The day was breaking. In the disfigured street

150. He left me, with a kind of valediction,

And faded on the blowing of the horn.

小吉丁
〈四重奏〉之四

對過去做過、有過的一切；

對事後才發覺的動機的可恥，以及

對做錯了而傷害到別人的一切的自覺

雖然你曾經認為這些舉動是美德。

145. 其次是愚人的贊同刺痛，而名譽沾汙。

從過錯到過錯，被激怒的靈魂

繼續，除非讓那地獄的淨火拯救回來，

在那兒你的動作必須按照尺度。一如舞蹈者。」

天快亮了。在面目不同的街頭

150. 他離我而去，以一種告別的方式，

而在號角的鳴聲中消失。

Little Gidding
No.4 of 'Four Quartets'

III

There are three conditions which often look alike

Yet differ completely, flourish in the same hedgerow:

Attachment to self and to things and to persons, detachment

155. From self and from things and from persons; and, growing

between them, Indifference

Which resembles the others as death resembles life,

Being between two lives—unflowering, between

The live and the dead nettle. This is the use of memory:

For liberation—not less of love but expanding

160. Of love beyond desire, and so liberation

From the future as well as the past. Thus, love of a country

Begins as attachment to our own field of action

And comes to find that action of little importance

小吉丁
〈四重奏〉之四

III

有三種狀態時常看起來很像

卻完全不同，繁茂在同一個籬牆：

依附自我、事物和人們，脫離

155. 自我、事物和人們；以及，在這兩者之間滋長的冷漠

類似對別人，有如死之對於生，

存在於兩種生命之間——不開花，

在活的和死的蕁麻之間。這是記憶的用處：

為了解放——不是愛的減少而是

160. 超越欲望的愛的擴大，因此

從未來乃至過去中解放出來。如此，對一個國家的愛

開始於對我們自己的行動領域的執著

進而發現，行動無關重要

Though never indifferent. History may be servitude,

165. History may be freedom. See, now they vanish,

The faces and places, with the self which, as it could, loved

them,

To become renewed, transfigured, in another pattern.

Sin is Behovely, but

All shall be well, and

170. All manner of thing shall be well.

If I think, again, of this place,

And of people, not wholly commendable,

Of no immediate kin or kindness,

But of some peculiar genius,

175. All touched by a common genius,

United in the strife which divided them;

小吉丁
〈四重奏〉之四

但絕不冷漠。歷史或許是奴役，

165. 歷史或許是自由。看吧，現在這些都消失而去，

那些臉、場所，與盡可能愛它們的自我一起

將獲得更新，變貌，以另一種樣式。

    罪是「無可逭」，可是

一切會是美好，而且

170. 凡事一切會是美好。

假如我再次想到這個地方，

以及人們，不完全是值得稱道，

亦無直接的親屬關係或親切感，

可是具有某種特殊的才能，

175. 大家都被一個共通的天才所感動，

在分裂他們的鬥爭中團結在一起；

Little Gidding
No.4 of 'Four Quartets'

If I think of a king at nightfall,

Of three men, and more, on the scaffold

And a few who died forgotten

180. In other places, here and abroad,

And of one who died blind and quiet

Why should we celebrate

These dead men more than the dying?

It is not to ring the bell backward

185. Nor is it an incantation

To summon the spectre of a Rose.

We cannot revive old factions

We cannot restore old policies

Or follow an antique drum.

190. These men, and those who opposed them

And those whom they opposed

小吉丁
〈四重奏〉之四

假如我想到一個國王在夜晚

想到三個人，甚至更多，在斷頭台上

以及有些人死去而被遺忘

180. 在別處，此地和國外，

想到一個眼瞎而默默死去的人，

為什麼我們要為這些

已死去的人而不是瀕死的人祝賀？

召喚玫瑰的幽魂

185. 既不是往後鳴鐘

也不是詛咒。

我們無法復活舊黨派

我們無法恢復舊政策

或者跟從古老的鼓聲。

190. 這些人，以及那些反對他們的人

和他們所反對的那些人，

Accept the constitution of silence

And are folded in a single party.

Whatever we inherit from the fortunate

195. We have taken from the defeated

What they had to leave us—a symbol:

A symbol perfected in death.

And all shall be well and

All manner of thing shall be well

200. By the purification of the motive

In the ground of our beseeching.

小吉丁

〈四重奏〉之四

　　接受沉默的制度

　　而被包括在單一的政黨中。

　　不論我們從幸運者中繼承了什麼

195.　我們從失敗者中得到了

　　他們不得不留給我們的──一個象徵：

　　以死達到完美的象徵。

　　而一切會是美好，而且

　　凡事一切會是美好

200.　藉著初心的淨化

　　在我們懇望的地下。

Little Gidding
No.4 of 'Four Quartets'

IV

The dove descending breaks the air

With flame of incandescent terror

Of which the tongues declare

205. The one discharge from sin and error.

The only hope, or else despair

    Lies in the choice of pyre or pyre—

    To be redeemed from fire by fire

    Who then devised the torment? Love.

210. Love is the unfamiliar Name

Behind the hands that wove

The intolerable shirt of flame

Which human power cannot remove.

小吉丁
〈四重奏〉之四

IV

鴿子從天而降衝破大氣

帶著白熱恐怖的火焰

以其舌頭宣示

205. 罪與過失的一個解脫。

唯一的希望，或者說絕望

　　就看這堆柴或那堆柴的選擇——

　　為了以火從火中獲得救贖。

　　那麼是誰設計了這種苦行？「愛」。

210. 「愛」是那個不熟悉的「名字」

在雙手背後編織

這難以忍受的火焰的襯衫

那是人的力量無法解脫的。

Little Gidding
No.4 of 'Four Quartets'

We only live, only suspire

215.   Consumed by either fire or fire.

小吉丁
〈四重奏〉之四

我們只能活下去，只能嘆息

215.　　被這火或那火焚燒殆盡。

Little Gidding
No.4 of 'Four Quartets'

V

What we call the beginning is often the end

And to make an end is to make a beginning.

The end is where we start from. And every phrase

And sentence that is right (where every word is at home,

220. Taking its place to support the others,

The word neither diffident nor ostentatious,

An easy commerce of the old and the new,

The common word exact without vulgarity,

The formal word precise but not pedantic,

225. The complete consort dancing together)

Every phrase and every sentence is an end and a beginning,

Every poem an epitaph. And any action

Is a step to the block, to the fire, down the sea's throat

小吉丁
〈四重奏〉之四

V

我們所謂的開始往往是結束

而著手結束亦即著手開始。

結束是我們開始的地方。每個適當的片語

和句子（其中每一字句都很舒適地

220. 以自己的位置支援別的字句，

這種字句既不心虛也不誇張，

舊詞和新語從容交易，

日常的字句精準不帶俗氣，

正式的字句準確而不賣弄學問，

225. 完美的伴侶在一起共舞）

每一字句都是一個結束，一個開始，

每一首詩是一篇墓誌銘。而一個動作

一個腳步，走向斷頭台，走向火，走入海的喉嚨

Or to an illegible stone: and that is where we start.

230. We die with the dying:

See, they depart, and we go with them.

We are born with the dead:

See, they return, and bring us with them.

The moment of the rose and the moment of the yew-tree

235. Are of equal duration. A people without history

Is not redeemed from time, for history is a pattern

Of timeless moments. So, while the light fails

On a winter's afternoon, in a secluded chapel

History is now and England.

240. With the drawing of this Love and the voice of this Calling

We shall not cease from exploration

And the end of all our exploring

小吉丁
〈四重奏〉之四

或者走向難以辨認的石碑：而這就是我們開始的地方。

230. 我們與瀕死的人一起死去：

看哪，他們走了，而我們跟隨他們。

我們與死者一起出生：

看哪，他們回來，帶著我們一起。

玫瑰的瞬間和紫杉樹的瞬間

235. 持續的時間相等。一個沒有歷史的民族

無法從時間中贖回，因為歷史是

諸多永恆瞬間的一個樣式。因此，當著陽光轉弱

在一個冬日的下午，一個僻靜的教堂，

歷史就是現在，且是英格蘭。

240. 以這種「愛」的引導和這種「感召」的聲音

　　我們不會停止探索

而我們所有探索的目的

Will be to arrive where we started

And know the place for the first time.

245. Through the unknown, remembered gate

When the last of earth left to discover

Is that which was the beginning;

At the source of the longest river

The voice of the hidden waterfall

250. And the children in the apple-tree

Not known, because not looked for

But heard, half-heard, in the stillness

Between two waves of the sea.

Quick now, here, now, always—

255. A condition of complete simplicity

(Costing not less than everything)

And all shall be well and

小吉丁
〈四重奏〉之四

是為了到達我們的出發點

而且初次認識那個地方。

245. 通過未知，記憶的門

當有待最後發現的土地

竟是曾經開始的地方；

在最長河流的源頭

隱蔽瀑布的聲音

250. 以及在蘋果樹中的孩子們

不為人知，因為未曾被尋找

但聽說過，半聽說過，在海上

兩個波浪之間的靜止中。

快，現在，此地，現在，無時無刻——

255. 一個全然純樸的的條件

（至少以所有的一切為代價）

而一切會是美好

Little Gidding
No.4 of 'Four Quartets'

All manner of thing shall be well

When the tongues of flame are in-folded

260. Into the crowned knot of fire

And the fire and the rose are one.

小吉丁
〈四重奏〉之四

凡事一切會是美好

當火焰的舌頭捲起

260. 結成火的王冠

而火和玫瑰合而為一。

1　譯註：小吉丁是位於英格蘭東劍橋郡的一個小社區，建於 17 世紀，歷史悠久，毀於戰火。

四重奏

2022年12月初版　　　　　　　　　　　定價：新臺幣620元
有著作權・翻印必究
Printed in Taiwan.

著　者	T. S. Eliot	
譯　者	杜　國　清	
校　對	吳　美　滿	
	吳　浩　宇	
整體設計	李　偉　涵	

出　版　者	聯經出版事業股份有限公司	副總編輯	陳　逸　華
地　　　址	新北市汐止區大同路一段369號1樓	總 編 輯	涂　豐　恩
叢書編輯電話	(02)86925588轉5319	總 經 理	陳　芝　宇
台北聯經書房	台北市新生南路三段94號	社　　長	羅　國　俊
電　　　話	(02)23620308	發 行 人	林　載　爵
台中辦事處	(04)22312023		
台中電子信箱	e-mail：linking2@ms42.hinet.net		
印　刷　者	世和印製企業有限公司		
總　經　銷	聯合發行股份有限公司		
發　行　所	新北市新店區寶橋路235巷6弄6號2樓		
電　　　話	(02)29178022		

行政院新聞局出版事業登記證局版臺業字第0130號

本書如有缺頁，破損，倒裝請寄回台北聯經書房更換。　　ISBN　978-957-08-6682-7（精裝）
聯經網址：www.linkingbooks.com.tw
電子信箱：linking@udngroup.com

國家圖書館出版品預行編目資料

四重奏/ T. S. Eliot著 . 杜國清譯 . 初版 . 新北市 . 聯經 .
2022年12月 . 160面 . 12.8×18.8公分
ISBN　978-957-08-6682-7（精裝）

873.51　　　　　　　　　　　　　　111019983